WARNING!

Scaredy Squirrel insists that
everyone check their heartbeat
before reading this book.

For XCW...

Library of Congress Cataloging-in-Publication Data is available upon request.
ISBN 978-0-593-30743-4 (hardcover)—
ISBN 978-0-593-30744-1 (lib. bdg.)—ISBN 978-0-593-30745-8 (ebook)

MANUFACTURED IN CHINA
10 9 8 7 6 5 4 3 2 1
First Edition

& FOR EVERY HEALTH CAREGIVER

Melanie Watt

Scaredy Squirrel

Visits the Doctor

Random House  New York

Scaredy Squirrel has never visited the doctor. He'd rather keep a healthy distance than risk going for a checkup. It might be a pain!

A few aches and pains Scaredy Squirrel is worried sick about:

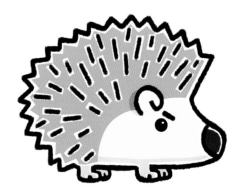

pricking

squeezing

head spinning

ear ringing

itching

poking

So he keeps his health in check to avoid visiting the doctor.

Scaredy stays fit by doing cardio workouts...

lifting weights...

NUTS ABOUT HEALTH

HEART

MUSCLES

balancing his diet ...

drinking milk ...

STOMACH ✓

BONES ✓

singing opera...

solving puzzles...

LUNGS ☑

BRAIN ☑

and taking good care
of his 5 senses.

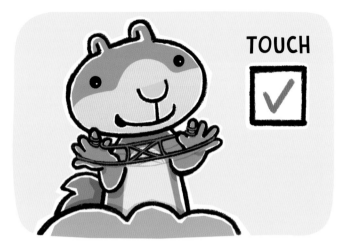

SMELL

HEARING

TASTE

SIGHT

DR. VET'S ADVICE:

EVERY ANIMAL SHOULD VISIT THE CLINIC TO GET A HEALTH CERTIFICATE!

IMPORTANT!
THIS PIECE OF PAPER IS PROOF THAT YOUR PET IS 100% HEALTHY!

Scaredy doesn't feel too good about seeing Dr. Vet.

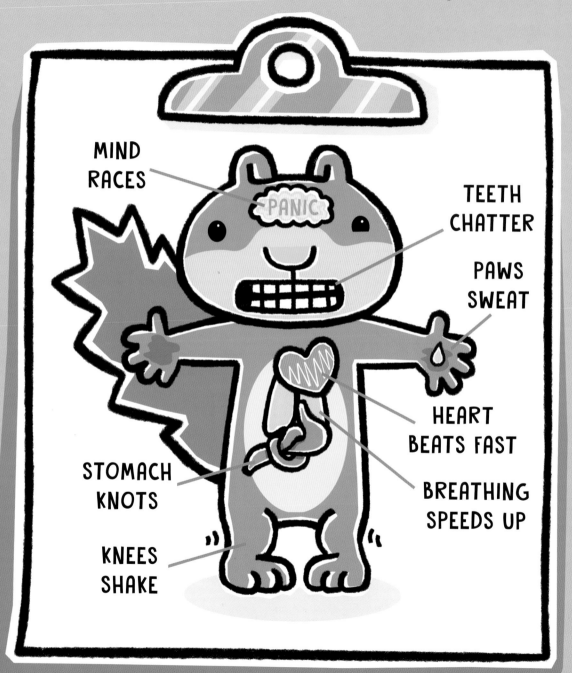

But having a certificate would put his mind at ease. So he plans a visit.

A few items Scaredy needs to safely visit Dr. Vet:

saw

pet carrier

bubble wrap

sweater

sunglasses

earplugs

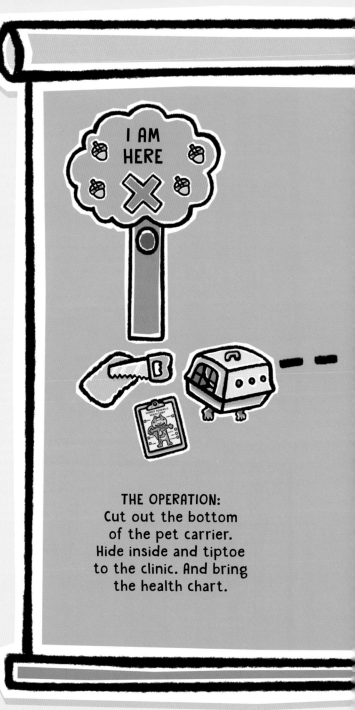

I AM HERE

THE OPERATION:
Cut out the bottom
of the pet carrier.
Hide inside and tiptoe
to the clinic. And bring
the health chart.

Wear sunglasses to bypass dizzying activity!

Flee if you see someone scratching excessively!

Put in earplugs to tune out ear-ringing noise!

1. SHOW HEALTH CHART.
2. WAIT FOR CERTIFICATE.
3. GO HOME AND FRAME IT.

Cover up with a warm sweater to shield self from air conditioning!

Use bubble wrap to avoid squeezing, pricking and poking!

If all else fails, play dead.

The next morning, Scaredy
carries out his plan.

He enters the clinic...

tiptoes into place...

sets up...and waits.

And waits...

When suddenly...

Being seen by Dr. Vet
was NOT part of the PLAN!

Scaredy Squirrel finally comes to his senses. Every patient here is in good hands.

looks at his X-ray...

FOOD GROUPS

explains how he can vary his meals...

and gives him an eye exam.

Scaredy sees it doesn't hurt at all to get a checkup. In fact, he feels good knowing everything is A-OK.

Last but not least, Dr. Vet has
helpful tips in case of panic...

Close your eyes...

think happy thoughts...

take deep breaths...

and try to relax.

LUNGS ✓

BODY ✓

Scaredy has never felt better!
He thanks Dr. Vet and helps
prepare everyone's certificates.

Dr. Vet congratulates Scaredy and tells him to keep up his healthy routine. Scaredy knows he can come back and visit anytime.

HEALTH CERTIFICATE

Scaredy Squirrel

Dr. Vet

Scaredy savors his
reward for days.
Then a letter arrives...

RELAXING
MUSIC

YOGA POSE

STRESS
BALL

P.S. A layer of bubble wrap never hurts!